PAPERCUTZ

MORE GREAT GRAPHIC NOVEL SERIES AVAILABLE FROM

PAPERCUTZ™

THE SMURFS #21

BRINA THE CAT #1

CAT & CAT #1

THE SISTERS #1

ATTACK OF THE STUFF

ASTERIX #1

SCHOOL FOR EXTRATERRESTRIAL GIRLS #1

GERONIMO STILTON REPORTER #1

THE MYTHICS #1

GUMBY #1

MELOWY #1

BLUEBEARD

THE RED SHOES

THE LITTLE MERMAID

FUZZY BASEBALL #1

HOTEL TRANSYLVANIA #1

THE LOUD HOUSE #1

MANOSAURS #1

THE ONLY LIVING BOY #5

THE ONLY LIVING GIRL #1

papercutz.com

Also available where ebooks are sold.

3: "Honestly, I Love My Sister"

Art and colors
William

Story
Cazenove & William

PAPERCUTZ

New York

To my grandparents: Lucette and André!

Thank you again, Christophe (the "joke incubator"); and to Olivier, for your trust.

Bravo, Arno, "ABI" for your "cast horse" joke and bravo, Noémie, for your "cast hold-all" joke.

A short note from Marine ("Maureen"): "Hey there, to all my friends, who I love so much, even if they're not all in my daddy's graphic novel."

A short note from Wendy: "I don't believe it)O_0...Now she's even crashing the acknowledgements page... ≷tsk, tsk, tsk...≷ What a goofball. But I love that little brat anyway ^ ^ !"

Don't copy any of the stunts shown in this graphic novel at home. The characters on these pages are overtrained and semi-pros at controlled falls ^ ^ !

—William

THE SISTERS #3 "Honestly, I Love My Sister"
Les Sisters [The Sisters] by Cazenove and William
© 2010, 2011 Bamboo Édition
Sisters, characters and related indicia are copyright, trademark and exclusive license of Bamboo Édition. English translation and all other editorial material
© 2017 by Papercutz
All rights reserved.

Story by Christophe Cazenove and William Maury
Art and color by William
Cover by William
Translation by Nanette McGuinness
Lettering by Wilson Ramos Jr.

For information address:
Bamboo Édition:
290 route des Allogneraies
71850 Charnay-Lès-Mâcon cedex FRANCE
bamboo@bamboo.fr – www.bamboo.fr

Papercutz books may be purchased for business or promotional use. For information on bulk purchases please contact Macmilan Corporate and Premium Sales Department at (800) 221-7945 x5442

Production — Dawn K. Guzzo
Editor — Robert V. Conte
Assistant Managing Editor — Jeff Whitman
Jim Salicrup
Editor-in-Chief

ISBN: 978-1-62991-645-3 Paperback Edition
ISBN: 978-1-62991-646-0 Hardcover Edition

Printed in India
November 2021

Distributed by Macmillan
Fourth Papercutz Printing

WHAT DID I TELL YOU, *MAUREEN?* LOOKS LIKE MORE *SPRING CLEANING* AND *VACUUMING* FOR US...

OH, NOOOO, *WENDY*-- HOUSEWORK MAKES ME BREAK OUT IN *HORROR-HIVES!*

YOU KNOW WHAT? THIS TIME, LET'S TRICK *MOM* AND *DAD!*

HA! THAT'S A GOOD IDEA!

OKAY, YOU'LL GO DOWN THE STAIRS AT *TOP SPEED...*

...AND I'LL CHASE AFTER YOU, *SCREAMING...*

...AS IF YOU'D BEEN GOING THROUGH MY ROOM... *THE USUAL DRILL...*

...THEN WE'LL QUICKLY CROSS THE LIVING ROOM AND *GET OUT OF THE HOUSE* BEFORE THEY CAN NAB US!

WOW... SUPER COOL PLAN!

OKAY, LET'S GO!

WAIT UNTIL I GIVE YOU THE START SIGNAL...

OKAY! TOTALLY READY WHEN YOU ARE!

3...2...1... — GO!

GERONIMO!

AH, MAUREEN! YOU'RE JUST *IN TIME.* HERE, GRAB THE VACUUM CLEANER AND HELP US FOR A WHILE...

HEE-HEE! IT'S SO AWESOME BEING THE *OLDEST!*

OH, NOOOO...UM, WENDYYY?

CAZENOVE & WILLIAM

HURRY UP, MAUREEN. WE CAN'T GO OUT WITH OUR FRIENDS IF THERE'S A SINGLE SPECK OF DUST LEFT IN OUR ROOMS.

YEAH... I HATE CHORES...

SLIPPPP...

HA-HA! SLIDING'S GREAT, ISN'T IT?

WAIT, I'LL ADD ANOTHER LAYER OF FOAM!

WATCH ME SKATE!

SLLLLIIIIDE...

YOUR TURN, WENDY!

THAT'S SO FUN!

CHECK THIS OUT--ISN'T IT AWESOME?!

DUST SPRAY

HA-HA! I'M DOING IT 20 TIMES BETTER THAN YOU!

BONK

DING A-DING DONG

UMM, GO ON WITHOUT US. WE HAVE A LOT OF CLEANING UP TO DO!

PLUS SKATING IS NOT REALLY OUR THING...

6

CAZENOVE & WILLIAM

DEAR DIARY: YOU KNOW, IF I HAD TO CHOOSE, THERE'S ONE OF MAUREEN'S FLAWS THAT SERIOUSLY GETS ON MY NERVES...

...SHE'S EXTREMELY NOISY!

RINNNGGGINGGG

I'LL GEEETTTT IT!

WHETHER SHE'S WATCHING HANNAH MATTRESS ON TV...

HA-HA-HA! MILEY CITRUS'S FACE!

...GULPING DOWN HER CHEESE, APRICOT AND BANANA SANDWICH...

EAT 5 PIECES OF FRUIT AND 5 VEGETABLES EVERY DAAAAY...

...DOING THE SHOPPING...

I PUSH THE CART SO I'M THE ONE WHO GETS TO CHOOSE THE ICE CREAM!

I GET TO! I GET TO!

I GET TO!

UH, MOM, CAN WE LOSE HER IN ONE OF THE AISLES?

...CHARGING DOWN THE STAIRS WEARING SOCKS AND SCREAMING THE WHOLE TIME...

GERONIMOOOOOOO...

BANGADANG

WELL, WHAT DO YOU KNOW? SHE'S ONLY QUIET WHEN SHE HURTS HERSELF!

BOO-HOO-HOOO

OH, WELL... IT WAS TOO GOOD TO BE TRUE!

CAZENOVE & WILLIAM

7

CAZENOVE & WILLIAM

MAUREEN, I'M HERE!

AND I'M HERE, TOO!

YOU'D NEVER KNOW IT, BUT IT'S *TOTALLY AWESOME* TO HAVE A LEG IN A CAST...

I'M YOUR *SERVANT.*

FOR STARTERS, IT'S *MAID-SERVANT!*

I'LL CARRY YOUR BOOK BAG.

POOH, YOU HAVE TROUBLE CARRYING YOUR OWN!

MY FRIENDS *LULU* AND *NAT* ARE SUPER SWEET TO ME...

MY DADDY WILL DRIVE US TO SCHOOL.

AFTER YOU, MY DEAREST FRIEND...

WE NEED TO PROP UP YOUR LEG NICELY ON THIS PILLOW.

THANKS!

LEAN ON ME, IF YOU'D LIKE.

ME TOO, ALWAYS!

YOU KNOW, I'LL *ALWAYS* BE HERE FOR YOU.

IT'S NICE TO KNOW YOU'VE GOT FRIENDS WHO'RE ALWAYS THERE FOR YOU...

SO... WHO'D LIKE TO ANSWER THE QUESTION?

MAUREEN?!

SO, MAUREEN, I'M LISTENING. DO YOU KNOW THE ANSWER?!

WELL, FRIENDS WHO'RE *ALMOST* ALWAYS THERE FOR YOU...

9

CAZENOVE & WILLIAM

THE GREAT THING ABOUT A CAST IS THAT YOU CAN'T RUN AROUND EVERYWHERE. SO YOU'VE GOT LOTS OF FREE TIME TO DREAM UP IDEAS FOR *PRACTICAL JOKES*...

...I HAD TONS OF 'EM FOR BUGGING *WENDY* THE WHOLE WEEK...

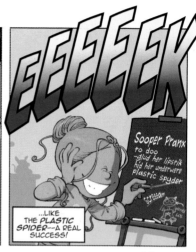

EEEEEK

...LIKE THE *PLASTIC SPIDER*--A REAL SUCCESS!

Sooper Pranx
to doo
-glud her lipstik
-hid her underwere
-plastic spyder

I WAS EXTRA PROUD OF THE *ITTY-BITTY HOLES* IN THE *MILK CARTON*...

...REPLACING THE SUGAR WITH SALT...

YUCK!

...AND PUTTING *GLUE* IN HER JAR OF MOUSSE...LOL! A GREAT LAUGH, BUT...

OOOOH, YOU...

NYAH-HA-HA-HA

...THE NOT-SO-GREAT THING ABOUT A CAST IS THAT YOU CAN'T *RUN.*

TUK TUK TUK TUK

CAZENOVE & WILLIAM

10

KNOCK-KNOCK! *ROOM SERVICE!*

KNOCK KNOCK

KNOCK

OKAY?

TOAST WITH *EMMIE'S* JAM AND *MOM'S* DIET SODA.

I'VE ALSO PEELED SOME MANDARIN ORANGES FOR YOU.

I'LL FLUFF THE PILLOWS A BIT SO THEY'RE MORE COMFORTABLE.

—THEEERE...

-PUFF-

-PUFF- -PUFF-

HERE YOU GO. I'M LENDING YOU MY MP3 PLAYER...

...AND MY NINTENDOX, TOO. IT'S GOT A NEW GAME THAT *AUDREY* PUT IN IT.

AND ABOVE ALL...

....DON'T FORGET THE MOST IMPORTANT THING!

OKAY, I'M GOING NOW BUT WILL BE NEAR THE DOOR IF YOU NEED ANYTHING ELSE. BYE-BYE!

WOW! MAUREEN'S A *SUPER* SISTER--

--YOU'RE SO *LUCKY!*

⸮PFFF...⸮ YEAH, SURE. LOOK AT WHAT SHE WROTE ON THE CAST...

UMM, IT LOOKS LIKE... *MATH?*

YUP... IT'S HER *BILL!*

C.CAZENOVE & WILLIAM

CAZENOVE & WILLIAM

WHERE'RE WE GOING, WENDY?

CLIMB ON, CURIOUS KID!

BUT... MY CRUTCHES?

DON'T WORRY, MAUREEN. WE'LL MANAGE!

≶PANT≶
≶PANT≶

≶PHEW≶
≶PHEW≶

HEE-HEE-HEE

≶PHEW≶
≶PHEW≶
≶PANT≶
≶PANT≶

≶HUFF≶ WE ≶PANT≶ ARE ≶PUFF≶ HERE...

THERE. DID ≶WHEEZE≶ YOU LIKE THE RIDE?

UMM, WELL...

GOOD. I'VE GOT SOMETHING IMPORTANT TO DO, SO I'LL LEAVE YOU HERE...

— BYE-BYE!

WOW ≶WHEEZE≶ HA-HA-HA... ≶PANT≶ HI, GIRLS...

AH, ARE WE GOING TO BE ABLE TO WATCH THAT NEW MOVIE ON MY LAPTOP?

DEFINITELY! WE'LL BE LEFT IN PEACE...

IT'LL TAKE HER AN HOUR-AND-A-HALF TO GET BACK HOME ON ONE LEG!

CAZENOVE & WILLIAM

THE HORSE IS A LARGE HERBIVOROUS, HOOFED MAMMAL THAT BELONGS TO ONE OF THE SEVEN SPECIES IN THE EQUINE FAMILY...

WHY DO YOU LOOK SO DOWN IN THE MOUTH, MAUREEN? YOU USUALLY LIKE SHOWS ABOUT HORSES!

YEAH, BUT WITH THIS CAST I WON'T BE RIDING A HORSE FOR A WHILE.

...THE MULE, THE RESULT OF CROSSING A DONKEY WITH A MARE, IS WELL KNOWN FOR ITS STRONG PERSONALITY...

I'VE GOT A GREAT IDEA! I'LL BE BACK... DON'T MOVE A MUSCLE!

RATS! I WAS ABOUT TO RUN OFF...

BONK

VZZZ GLOP

TAP

FITCH

?

HERE WE GO!

I'M COMING! I'M COMING!

AH, BUT...

...NO...

BUT YES!

NO... WENDY!

WAIT!

YOUR THINGIE IS TOTALLY LAME!

⸮GRRR...⸗ MAUREEN, YOU'RE NEVER HAPPY!

GO ON AND SULK THEN––THAT'S A COOL HOBBYHORSE!

HAS ANYONE SEEN THE STRAP FOR MY PURSE?

ABi, CAZENOVE & WILLIAM

SIGH

HEY! WHAT'S WITH THE GLOOMY MUG?

DADDY'S GOING TO TAKE ME TO THE HOSPITAL SO THEY CAN TAKE OFF MY CAST.

LOL! YOU KNOW YOU RARELY GET TO KEEP THAT KIND OF THING FOR LIFE.

OH, HA-HA. DID YOU *SWALLOW A CLOWN* THIS MORNING?

DO YOU THINK THEY'LL HAVE TO BREAK IT?

OF COURSE! IT'S NOT A SOCK, YOU KNOW.

BUT LOOOK HOW PREEETTY IT IS...ALL MY FRIENDS DREW ON IT. AND ALSO *DADDY* AND *MOMMY* AND *YOU* AND EVEN *DARWIN*.

WHATEVS

UNLESS...

YAY. I HAVE A GREAT IDEA! HEE-HEE!

WHERE'RE YOU GOING? YOU KNOW DAD DOESN'T LIKE YOU HANGING OUT IN HIS OFFICE.

BUT I JUST WANT TO SCAN THE DRAWINGS!

LOL! A CAST FOR *YOUR BRAIN* IS WHAT YOU NEED...!

15

CAZENOVE & WILLIAM

I'M NOT HAPPY AT ALL, *WENDY!*

YEAH, NOT HAPPY AT ALL!

IT'S PAST TIME FOR YOU TO SETTLE DOWN AND FLY RIGHT.

YEAH, GET DOW AND FLY A KITE.

NEXT TIME, YOU'LL THINK TWICE BEFORE YOU MISBEHAVE.

YEAH, MAYBE EVEN THREE TIMES.

YOU UNDERSTAND THAT I MUST PUT MY FOOT DOWN.

YEAH, BUT I HAVE TO PUT MY FEET UP.

YOU'LL SET THE TABLE EVERY DAY FOR A MONTH!

UM...*MOM*... WOULDN'T YOU RATHER FIND *ANOTHER* PUNISHMENT?

WHAT? NO! WILL THAT BRAT SHUT HER TRAP?!

WAM

TAKE SOMETHING AWAY FROM HER. HER TELEPHONE OR NINTENDOX. SOMETHING LIKE THAT, YOU KNOW?!

HOW DO YOU EXPECT MY *PANDY* TO SET THE TABLE?

OH, COME ON, FIND ANOTHER PUNISHMENT. *PLEEEZE*....?

NO MATTER WHAT, WHEN *MAUREEN'S* IN TROUBLE, SHE SHARES THE PUNISHMENT WITH HER *STUFFED ANIMALS!*

CAZENOVE & WILLIAM

WHAT CAN YOU DO? I'M TELLING YOU, SAMMIE...

IT'S A CURSE!

I HUNG OUT AFTER SCHOOL INSTEAD OF DOING MY HOMEWORK. MY PC WAS TAKEN AWAY...

I LET SOME CURSE WORDS FLY AND MY PHONE WAS TAKEN AWAY...

I LEFT MY ROOM A MESS FOR A WEEK. MY NINTENDOX WAS TAKEN AWAY...

I BROUGHT HOME A TON OF BAD GRADES AND GOT GROUNDED...

...AND MY ALLOWANCE WAS TAKEN AWAY FOR... *ACTING OUT* AGAINST *MAUREEN*.

I SWEAR TO YOU, I'VE REALLY TRIED *EVERYTHING*...

...BUT NOT *ONCE* HAS MY SISTER BEEN TAKEN AWAY!

CAZENOVE & WILLIAM

WENDY, WENDY, WENDY! WANT TO KNOW SOMETHING CRAZY?

— NO!

COME OOOON...YESSSS, YOU DO...IT'S SO AWESOOOOME!

YOU KNOW HOW YESTERDAY, MOM DIDN'T WANT TO BUY ME THOSE CHOCOLATE SHOES...? AND, WELL, DO YOU KNOW WHAT I DID?

YOU HOWLED LIKED A CAR ALARM. NO NEWS THERE!

NOPE, NOPE. YOU LOSE.

I JUST CLICKED MY HEELS AND CLAPPED MY HANDS TOGETHER HARD... ...LIKE THIS!

WHATEVS!

TSK...!!

THUMP
THUMP
THUMP

AND I GOT MY CHOCOLATE SHOES! HA-HA!

AND LATER, WHEN I GOT JAM ON DADDY'S DRAWINGS...

...SAME THING... HE DIDN'T SEE ANYTHING!

IT'S MAGIC! I HAVE A SPELL FOR WHEN I'M GOING TO HAVE BAD LUCK!

BAD LUCK!

YAHOOO!

I'M MAGICALLLL! NA-NA-NA-NA-NNNNNA!

SO TELL ME, DIDN'T YOU HAVE A POEM TO LEARN?

THE POEM!

SOOOO...DID YOU LEARN THAT POEM, MAUREEN?

UH–UMM...ANY SECOND NOW, MA'AM...

PAT

PAT

PAT

TUNK

TUNK
TUNK
TUNK

CAZENOVE x WILLIAM

CAZENOVE & WILLIAM

YOU'D NEVER KNOW IT, BUT *WENDY* IS TOTALLY *OCD*...

♪ BABY
BABY BABY OOOH

OH, NOT WAY! MY *CDs* GO BACK INTO THEIR CASE AND PUT THAT DOWN BEFORE IT *BREAKS!*

♪ BABY
BABY OOH

TOTALLY OCD. AT BREAKFAST, TOO...

YUCK! KEEP YOUR CRUMBS ON YOUR SIDE ALREADY!

SMACK
CRACK
YUM

SHE HAS A FIT WHEN I TOUCH HER THINGS...

I KNEW IT! YOU *NEVER* PUT THE CAPS BACK ON MY MARKERS... THEY'RE ALL GOING TO DRY OUT! ⸮GRRR...⸮ DIMWIT!

SHE EVEN BLOWS A FUSE WHEN I PLAY WITH MY TOYS...

THIS IS A FAMILY ROOM, NOT A *ZOO!*

HEEEYYY... YOU HURT *FAIRYZILLA...*

TORTURER!

STILL...

...THERE'RE TIMES SHE'S NOT OCD AT ALL!

HURRY, HURRY-- MASON'S INVITED ME TO THE MOVIEEEES...

YEAH, WELL, DON'T COUNT ON *ME* TO CLEAN UP *YOUR* THINGS!

*OCD: OBSESSIVE-COMPULSIVE DISORDER, IS A MENTAL DISORDER THAT WENDY DOES *NOT* HAVE. IT'S A SERIOUS PROBLEM, NOT TO BE TAKE LIGHTLY. MAUREEN DOESN'T UNDERSTAND THAT, BUT NOW YOU *DO!*

CAZENOVE & WILLIAM

COME ON, *WENDY*, TELL ME, TELL ME, TELL ME...

PRETTY PLEASE, PRETTY PLEASE, PRETTY PLEASE...

≳GRRR≲ LEAVE ME ALONE, YOU GLUE STICK!

BESIDES, IT'S NONE OF YOUR BEESWAX FOR STARTERS!

PRETTY PLEASE, WENDY...

...I REALLY WANT TO KNOW WHAT IT MEANS TO BE IN LOVE.

≳HMMPH≲ OKAY, BUT KEEP IT TO YOURSELF.

CROSS YOUR HEART AND HOPE TO DIE, STICK A NEEDLE IN YOUR EYE!

PINKY SWEAR. I WON'T SAY A THING!

PTOOFY

THE THING IS THAT *MASON* AND I ARE *INTENSELY CLOSE*...

...BUT IT STAYS *PLATONIC*, YOU KNOW. YOU CAN'T IMAGINE THIS...

...BUT WE'RE MADE FOR EACH OTHER.

A SIMPLE GLANCE GIVES BIRTH TO ROMANTIC FIREWORKS...

...BUT OUR RELATIONSHIP IS EVER-CHANGING, PRETTY MUCH.

IT'S WILD...

...SUPER CALM, THEN A TORRENT OF PASSION, FOLLOWED BY A LULL.

???

YOU'RE JUST A *BIG JERK*, MASON... YOU'VE BROKEN MY SISTER...

I CAN'T UNDERSTAND A WORD SHE SAYS NOW!

CAZENOVE & WILLIAM

WENDYYY... I FOUND LOTS OF *SCI-ANTI-FIG* EXPERIMENTS!

HAVE YOU NOTICED BEFORE THAT THE "S" IN THE WORD *"SNAIL"* IS MARKED ON ITS SHELL?

WOW!

WAIT, THAT'S NOT ALL!

WHEN YOU DUNK A ROLL OF PAPER TOWELS COMPLETELY INTO A TUB OF WATER, IT ABSORBS ALL THE LIQUID!

OH, MY GOSH!

AND WITH A BALLOON, DO YOU KNOW WHAT?

YOU PUT A *BAN-DAID* ON IT AND IT WON'T *BURST.*

⸘PHEW...⸘

AND BEST OF ALL IS THE *SOFT MUSIC* YOU CAN MAKE WITH A *PEN CAP!*

UH, WELL.

I'M GOING TO DO LOTS MORE OF THEM, THEN I WILL BE IN THE *ONE-CYCLOPEDIA* OF SCIENTISTS!

YEAH, YEAH... SURE, SURE...

!

LOOK AT *THIS*-- IT'S SO *STRONG*...

...A KEY IN THE SHAPE OF A HAMMER THAT OPENS EVERY LOCK!

CAZENOVE & WILLIAM

AFTER HEAPS AND HEAPS OF MATHEMATICAL CALCULATIONS, I FINALLY UNDERSTAND HOW *WENDY* WORKS...

WITH MY SISTER, HER MOOD CHANGES EVERY OTHER DAY...

THE PROOF? YESTERDAY, SHE WAS DIETING...

A SALAD AND A GLASS OF WATER, *DAD*. DIET, YOU KNOW...

AND TODAY, WITH HER BUDS, SHE STUFFED HER FACE LIKE AN *OGRE!*

THIS BARBECUE SAUCE IS SOOO GOOD!

SLURP

YOU WANT TO FINISH MY FRIES?

YESTERDAY HER HAIR IS TOTALLY *AWFUL*, TODAY *IT'S* THE PRETTIEST IN THE WORLD...

...WHICH SHOWS THAT SHE CHANGES HER MIND *EVERY OTHER DAY*...

SO, SINCE I GOT REJECTED YESTERDAY...

WENDY, WILL YOU GIVE ME YOUR *PRIVATE DIARY?* I HAVEN'T FINISHED READING IT.

WELL, OKAY, IT'S NOT *ALWAYS* EVERY OTHER DAY...!

CAZENOVE & WILLIAM

PSSST

WENDY. HEY, WENDY...

...I'M A LITTLE *COLD!*

...*MMPH*... ...*MMMOOUMPH*... I-IT'S OKAY...

THANKS-- YOU'RE *COOL!*

SLEEPING IN MY BED, OKAY! STEALING MY COMFORTER-- *NOT OKAYYYYY!*

24

CAZENOVE & WILLIAM

WHENEVER THERE'S A STORM, *MAUREEN* BECOMES *UNBEARABLE*...

BROOOOOOOOOOOOOOOOOO

OH, NOOOO...

SHE THROWS A HISSY FIT AND BAYS AT THE MOON...

THE LIGHTNING'S GOING TO FRY US ALL!

YOU KNOW, *MAUREEN*, I REALLY *LIKE* STORMS!

THAT'S 'CUZ THE LIGHTNING'S FRIED YOUR *BRAIN!*

LISTEN TO THE SOUND OF THE RAIN ON THE ROOF...

KAPOOM

ISN'T IT PLEASANT? AND THE GRAY SKY OUTSIDE...

I LOVE THIS AMBIENCE!

IF THE POWER GOES OUT, WE LIGHT LOTS OF CANDLES...

WHICH SMELL GOOD!

AND WE PLAY BOARD GAMES WAITING FOR IT TO BE OVER.

AH... YEAH!

SO, ISN'T ALL THAT GREAT?

TOTALLY!

BUT SHE'S *STILL* UNBEARABLE!

IT'S SO GREEEAAT!

WHEN'S THE NEXT STORM? WHEN IS IT?

WHEEEEN...?!

CAZENOVE & WILLIAM

CAZENOVE & WILLIAM

I SWEAR TO YOU, *AUDREY,* I'VE FINALLY FOUND AN *ANTI-SISTER REPELLENT!*

AWWWESOME... TELL ME ABOUT IT, *WENDY!*

IT'S SOMETHING CRAZY. I TOSSED *THREE STINKY BALLS* AROUND MY BED.

HA-HA... THAT'S *EXTREME!*

WENDYYYY...

EXACTLY. HERE'S THE LITTLE *TWIRP,* THIS IS GOING TO BE FUNNY...

BAM!

SNIFF   SNIFF

SNIFF   SNIFF

YUCK! WHAT IS THAT *ROTTEN SMELL?*

LOL YEAHHH!

I'M NOT STEPPING IN HERE ANYMORE.

EW!

OH, BY THE WAY, I CAME TO TELL YOU YOUR *MASEY-WASEY'S* HERE.

NOoO ?!

WENDY... YOO-HOO, ARE YOU THERE?

PSHEEEEE

PSHEEEEE

PSHEEEEE

YES, UH, NO, UH, WAIT, *MASON...* I... >GRRR...<

>SNIFF< ARE YOU SICK? >PEW<

27

CAZENOVE & WILLIAM

CAZENOVE & WILLIAM

WOOOW!

REALLY? IS IT TRUE? IT'S FOR *ME*?!

I CAN'T BELIEVE IT! IT'S SO PRETTY-- WOOOOWWW--WHAT A PRESENT!

YOU CAN OPEN IT, YOU KNOW!

WHAT IS IT?

LOL

SCRATCH

SCRITCH

SCRITCH

WOOOOWW!

Your Diary
PRIVATE
M

A *DIARY*... JUST FOR ME?!

I LOVE YOU SO MUCH, MY DEAR SISTER!

THIS WAY YOU WON'T STEAL MINE ANYMORE.

I'VE GOT A PRIINAAATE DIARY...

I'VE GOT A PRIINAAATE DIARY...

A LITTLE LATER...

LET'S SEE HOW THE "WRITER'S" FARING...

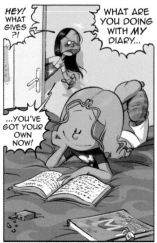

HEY! WHAT GIVES?!

WHAT ARE YOU DOING WITH *MY* DIARY...

...YOU'VE GOT YOUR OWN NOW!

WELL, I'M READING YOURS FOR *IDEAS* WHAT I SHOULD WRITE IN MINE...

29

CAZENOVE & WILLIAM

USUALLY, IT GOES LIKE *THIS*...

SNORE

MAUREEN, MAUREEN-- WAKE UP!

...WHEN OUR PARENTS TAKE US SOMEWHERE, WE LET MY SISTER KNOW AT THE LAST MINUTE...

...BECAUSE AS SOON AS SHE KNOWS, SHE BECOMES *INFURIATING*...

COME ON, GET UP. WE'RE GOING TO SPEND THE DAY AT THE AQUATIC PARK!

TO THE AT QUACK DUCK PARK?

FOR REAL?

YEP, THAT'S RIGHT.

YEEEAAAAHHHOOOOOOOOO!

I LOVE THE *AT QUACK DUCK PARK!*

TOTALLY AWESOME!

THEY'VE GOT WATER SLIDES!

I''LL GET TO GO ON ALL-NEW RIDES!

I NEED MY SUNSCREEN!

I NEED MY HANNAH MATTRESS SWIMSUIT!

MY SWIMSUIT! MY SWIMSUIT! MY SWIMSUIT!

THIS TIME, I LET HER KNOW 15 HOURS IN *ADVANCE*...

WENDYYYYY... COME HERE RIGHT NOW!

MY SWIMSUIT!

THAT'LL TEACH MOM AND *DAD* TO STOP ME FROM GOING TO THE MOVIES WITH MY BUDS!

HEH-HEH!

CAZENOVE & WILLIAM

CAZENOVE & WILLIAM

Y'KNOW, LAST NIGHT I MADE A *PACT* WITH *MOM* AND *DAD*.

A *PACT?!* DO YOU EVEN KNOW WHAT THAT WORD MEANS?

UH-HUH! I PROMISED TO WORK SUPER HARD AT SCHOOL, AND YOU KNOW WHAT?

DON'T CARE.

COME ON, GUESS, GUESS, GUESS...

IN EXCHANGE, THEY OFFERED ME A *WOOEE* WITH A GAME AND JOYSTICKS!

HEH-HEH

HAH... YOU'VE SO BEEN *HAD!*

WHY DO YOU SAY THAT? THEY CAN'T LIE. THEY'RE *GROWNUPS!*

WELL, WHEN I WAS YOUR AGE I ALSO CAME TO AN AGREEMENT WITH OUR PARENTS...

AND?

THEY PROMISED ME THAT IF I WAS WELL-BEHAVED, I'D HAVE THE NICEST, CUTEST LITTLE SISTER...

WE BOTH KNOW HOW *THAT* TURNED OUT, SO I WOULDN'T TRUST THEIR PROMISES...!

HEE-HEE

=HUMPH=

CAZENOVE & WILLIAM

MAUREEN'S REALLY PATHETIC WITH HER *MR. BUN BUN...*

SO WHAT COLOR WAS HENRY IV'S *WHITE HORSE?*

YOU HAVEN'T DONE YOUR HOMEWORK!

SHE ACTS AS IF HE WERE *ALIVE...*

...AND A NICE PIECE OF TOAST WITH APRICOT AND BUTTER...

...WHICH YOU LOVE SO MUCH!

MOMMY, MR. BUN BUN FINISHED HIS SNACK AND HE REALLY LIKED IT!

IT'S MR. BUN BUN WHO MADE THIS MESS, *DADDY!*

I'M GOING TO PUNISH HIM!

IT'S JUST SO RIDICULOUS. ONE DAY I WILL TELL HER THAT MR. BUN BUN IS NOTHING MORE THAN A *STUFFED ANIMAL.*

KA-KRASH!

I *SWEAR* TO YOU. I DON'T KNOW WHAT GOT INTO MR. BUN BUN...HE HOPPED ONTO THE LAMP LIKE A *LUNATIC!*

≈MMFFF≈
≈MMMM...≈

CAZENOVE & WILLIAM

CAZENOVE & WILLIAM

CAZENOVE & WILLIAM

AND THERE'S *FAIRYZILLA*, WHO DESTROYS THE CASTLE OF THAT ROTTEN *PRINCE CHARMING*...

KABLAM

MAUREEEN!

DID YOU HAVE TO TELL *MOM* AND *DAD* THAT I GOT AN F IN MATH?!

I CAN'T BELIEVE IT...

SCREECH

...YOU'RE JUST A *TATTLE-TELLING* SNEAKER!

IT'S YOUR FAULT I HAVE TO CLEAN THE HOUSE FOR THE NEXT MONTH...

...AND I CAN'T USE MY COMPUTER, EITHER!

WHEN IT COMES TO BIG SNEAKS, YOU'RE SO BIG, YOU'RE *OFF-THE-SCALE* BIG!

NOT TRUE! NOT TRUE! NOT TRUUUE!

I'D RATHER LEAVE THE HOUSE THAN STAY INSIDE WITH THE *QUEEN OF BIG SNEAKS!*

I KNEW SHE WAS *WRONG!*

MY WEIGHT IS *NOT* OFF-THE-SCALE!

CAZENOVE & WILLIAM

EMMA'S MY SISTER WENDY'S NEW DANCE BUDDY...

ALL RIGHT, I'M READY.

WE'RE GOING TO HAVE A BLAST WITH THIS CHOREOGRAPHY!

...BUT I DON'T LIKE EMMA.

BY THE WAY, I'VE BROUGHT YOU THE CD WE'LL BE DANCING TO...

COOL!

...AND YOU'LL SEE THERE'S SOME SONGS BY JUSTIN BABY THERE, TOO.

WOW--I'M SO INTO HIM. I CAN'T WAIT TO DANCE TO THEM!

I'M HIS BIGGEST FAN!

⋍PFFFF...⋍ WHAT A SHOW-OFF!

MY COUSIN MAY BE A BIGGER ONE. SHE TRAVELLED ALL OVER THE STATES TO SEE HIM ON TOUR.

REALLY? WISH I COULD DO THAT!

I WISH YOU WOULD LEAVE AND TRAVEL THE SKATES, TOO.

MY LITTLE SISTER'S GOING TO COME WATCH US DANCE. YOU'LL MEET HER.

SHE'S ADORABLE!

⋍MMM...?⋍

FINALLY SOMEONE WHO LIKES LITTLE SISTERS!

WELL, YOU'VE MET MINE ALREADY...

CAZENOVE & WILLIAM

YOU WON'T FORGET MY BIRTHDAY PARTY THIS SATURDAY, RIGHT *WENDY*?

NO WAY! I ALREADY KNOW WHAT I'M GOING TO WEAR...

A BIRTHDAY PARTAY?!

I LOVE THOSE SO MUCH...

...BUT MS. BOSSY BOOTS NEVER LETS ME GO WITH HER!

UNLESS ...

TA-DAH...

WHO'S *THIRSTY*?

CHERRY SODA...

...COOK-A-KOLA...

...AND EVEN ICE CUBES!

...FANTEE...

I'D REALLY LIKE A KOLA, *MAUREEN*.

SAY, WOULD *YOU* LIKE TO COME TO MY BIRTHDAY PARTY, TOO?

I'M INVITED...? FOR REALS?!

OF *COURSE*!

HAVING FUN, WENDY?

HA-HA-HA, TOTALLY! I'VE NEVER HAD SUCH A GREAT TIME IN *MY LIFE*!

CAZENOVE & WILLIAM

CAZENOVE & WILLIAM

CAZENOVE & WILLIAM

BEEP BEEP BEEP BEEP BEEP

:YAAAWWWN...:

BEEP BEEP BEEP BEEP BEEP

:GRUMPH!: WHAT IS THAT *NOISE?!*

IS THAT YOUR ALARM, MAUREEN?

WELL, I'VE GOT SCHOOL TODAY.

SO DO I, BUT IT'S *FOUR O'CLOCK IN THE MORNING!*

BEEP
CLICK

I'VE GOT LOTS OF ODDS-AND-ENDS TO TAKE CARE OF...

SCRATCH-SCRATCH

YOU MEAN *IN ADDITION* TO KEEPING ME FROM SLEEPING?!

BEFORE TAKING MY BATH, *I* HAVE TO GET *MR. BUN BUN* READY...

...BRUSH HIM, COMB HIM AND PUT COLOGNE ON HIM.

THAT ONLY TAKES YOU *FIVE MINUTES*--

--YOU DON'T NEED TO GET UP SO CRAZY EARLY!

NO, BUT DO YOU THINK I'VE ONLY GOT MR. BUN BUN TO TAKE CARE OF?!

41

CAZENOVE & WILLIAM

YIIIKES...!
TELL ME YOU *DIDN'T* JUST DO THAT!

YUP, I ALSO BROKE ANOTHER BOTTLE OF *DADDY'S* INDIA INK BUT BE *QUIET!* HE'S GOING TO HEEEAAAR...

SHHHH...

OKAY, BUT I TOLD YOU *NOT* TO CRAWL AROUND IN HIS OFFICE!

PSHEEEE...

DON'T TELL HIM, OKAY?

WE'LL *SEE...*

WENDY?! YOU WON'T SAY ANYTHING, *RIGHT?*

SURE, BUT ONLY ON *ONE* CONDITION...

...YOU'LL SET THE TABLE FOR ME FOR A MONTH...

MMMM... FINE!

...THEN I'LL HAVE YOUR COMPUTER TIME FOR A WHOLE WEEK...

...YOU'LL MAKE MY BED, TOO...

PSHEEE...

...YOU WON'T GO INTO MY ROOM ANYMORE, ESPECIALLY WHEN MY FRIENDS ARE HERE...

§GRUMPH!§

PSHEEEE...

YEAH YEAH YEAH

...YOU WON'T TOUCH MY MAKEUP CASE...

...AND, FINALLY, YOU'LL GIVE ME YOUR CHOCOLATE MO--

--AAAH!

WHAT'RE YOU DOING, NOW?!

WELL, SINCE I AGREE TO ALL YOUR DEMANDS, I'M GOING TO MISBEHAVE TO THE *MAX!*

CAZENOVE & WILLIAM

CAZENOVE & WILLIAM

CAZENOVE & WILLIAM

CAZENOVE & WILLIAM

UMM... YOU'RE SURE YOUR SISTER ISN'T AROUND?

IF SHE SEES US, WE'RE *DEAD!*

IF *WENDY* ISN'T IN FRONT OF THE TV, IN FRONT OF THE MIRROR, OR IN FRONT OF THE FRIDGE, IT'S BECAUSE SHE ISN'T HERE!

AND NOW, WELCOME TO WENDYLAND!

SO CLASSY!

I LOVE HER BED!

LOOK AT THE THREADS SHE'S GOT!

LOOK, MAUREEN, I'M A REAL *ADOLESCENT.*

LOL! YOU'RE JUST MISSING PIMPLES ON YOUR FACE!

HER MUSIC'S GREAT!

YUP. IT'S AARON BEE!

YO- YO- | OYO!

AND LOOK AT ALL THE DVDS SHE'S—

MAUREEN, WHERE ARE YOU *GOING?* YOU DON'T WANT TO GO THROUGH YOUR SISTER'S THINGS ANYMORE?

YES, LULU, BUT I'M CALLING HER SO THAT SHE'LL COME BACK...

...IT'S MUCH *LESS FUN* WHEN YOU KNOW YOU CAN'T *GET CAUGHT!*

46

CAZENOVE & WILLIAM

WHAT ARE ALL THESE *FIBS?!*

DID YOU MESS UP MY DIARY OR WHAT?!

YOU WERE SUPPOSED TO LEARN THAT POEM TODAY. IT'S REALLY NO BIG DEAL...

AND YOU DON'T KNOW IT EITHER, *PANDY?*

WELL, THAT'S JUST GREAT!

DO YOU HAVE A NOTE FROM YOUR PARENTS?

NOT EVEN THAT?

≳PFFF...≲ YES, I'VE GOT A BUNCH OF *IGNORE AMUSES.*

YOU DIDN'T HAVE ENOUGH TIME? YEAH, SURE...I DON'T BELIEVE YOU.

DON'T PUSH IT...

IT'S BEEN A WEEK SINCE I TOLD YOU THERE'D BE A SURPRISE QUIZ!

NOW YOU MAY STAND IN THE CORNER...

THAT'LL TEACH YOU TO IGNORE YOUR ASSIGNMENTS!

MAUREEN, YOU GOT A *ZERO!*

NOW YOU MAY STAND IN THE CORNER... THAT'LL TEACH YOU TO IGNORE YOUR ASSIGNMENTS!

COPYCAT!

CAZENOVE & WILLIAM

CAZENOVE & WILLIAM

WHEN I WANT TO TELL SOMEONE A SECRET, I'VE GOT **LOTS** OF CHOICES...

...OF COURSE, THERE'S MY SISTER **WENDY** AND I KNOW SHE WON'T TELL EVEN HER BEST BUDS...

IT'S THE SAME WITH **MOMMY.** WHEN I TELL HER A SECRET, IT'S SAFER THAN THE HUGEST SAFE FILLED WITH CASH ON EARTH!

BILL

...DADDY WOULDN'T SAY ANYTHING EITHER...

BESIDES, I'M NOT EVEN SURE HE EVEN REMEMBERS THEM.

CREAK

ZZZ

THEN THERE'S **MR. BUN BUN**... I TOTALLY TRUST HIM.

BUT IN GENERAL, I TELL MY BIGGEST SECRETS TO **NAT.**

WHISPER WHISPER WHISPER

NOOO?!

YES!

HONESTLY, WHAT'S THE POINT OF HAVING A SECRET IF NO ONE KNOWS ABOUT IT?!

WHISPER WHISPER WHISPER

CAZENOVE & WILLIAM

BLAH BLAH BLAH   BLAH BLAH

AND SO ON AND SO FORTH

DID THEY REALLY STOP TALKING BECAUSE OF ME?

HMM... I'LL TRY AGAIN...

YOU'RE REALLY ROTTEN!

AND MEAN!

AND IT'S ALL 'CUZ YOU'RE PLOTTING AGAINST ME, RIGHT?!

I HAAAATE ALL OF YOU!

DO YOU STILL WANT US TO COME UP WITH AN IDEA FOR A BIRTHDAY PRESENT FOR MAUREEN?

NO WAY!

CAZENOVE & WILLIAM

HAVING **WENDY** IN A CLOTHING STORE IS TOTALLY **AWFUL**...

YEAH!

GO CLASSY!

Saint Felix Town

...SHE TAKES THREE YEARS TO MAKE UP HER MIND...

UH, **SAMMIE**--IN YOUR OPINION?

TRY ON **ALL** OF THEM. THAT'LL BE EASIEST!

AND HA-HA-HAH-HA-HA, THE SCARF IS TOO LONG...

MEH!

DON'T WORRY, WE'LL FIGURE IT OUT!

...AND THE JACKET, HA-HA-HAH-HA-HA, IT'S TOO BLUE...⸮PFFF⸮...

YUCK. THE COLOR KILLS THE STYLE!

AND THE **SHOES**, HA-HA-HAH-HA-HA, THE LACES ARE TOO BIG...

WENDY, DO YOU WANT TO CATCH A MOVIE TONIGHT?

FRESH Girl

A MOVIE?! I'LL GO!

I'LL GO! I'LL GO! I'LL GO! I'LL GO! HEY, WENDY, MAY I GO?!

NO!

YEAH, WELL, SOMETIMES SHE MAKES UP HER MIND **TOO QUICKLY**!

CAZENOVE & WILLIAM

AH, YOU'RE HERE, **WENDY**...

...I WAS LOOKING **EVERYWHERE** FOR YOU!

I'M GOING TO GIVE YOU A PRESENT. BUT FIRST, YOU HAVE TO PROMISE TO KEEP IT.

=MMMNNN=...
=GRUMPH=...

YOU'RE NOT ALLOWED TO THROW IT **OUT**, PUT IT **DOWN**, GIVE IT **AWAY**, OR PUT IT IN YOUR PURSE, OKAY?

OTHERWISE, IT'S NOT WORTH IT.

=SIGH=

TA-DAAAH!

AND HEEEERE IT IS...A PRESENT FOR YOU!

HONESTLY! YOU THINK THAT--

YOU **PROMISED**. YOU HAVE TO HOLD IT IN YOUR HAND, ALWAYS!

ARE WE GOOD?!

YES, HEE-HEE-HEE...

SHE DOESN'T SUSPECT A THING. WE'LL HEAR **EVERYTHING** MY SISTER AND HER BOYSFRIEND SAY!

I BROUGHT SOMETHING TO TAKE NOTES WITH!

ARE YOU **AN ONLY CHILD**, I HOPE?!

CAZENOVE & WILLIAM

CAZENOVE & WILLIAM

WENDY HAS A SUPER-STRANGE OBSESSION-- SHE ONLY EATS TOMATOES...

...NOTHING AT DINNER EXCEPT THE ONES SHE JUGGLES AND SWALLOWS...

CHOMP YUM CHOMP

AND FOR DESSERT, WHAT DOES SHE EAT? A BOWL OF CHERRY TOMATOES... EVEN WHEN WE'VE GOT CHOCOLATE CAKE...

SHE DOESN'T EVEN GIVE THEM TIME TO RIPEN IN THE GARDEN...

AAAH! LOVELY!

MAUREEN, GO GET YOUR SISTER TO CLEAR THE TABLE, PLEASE.

YES, MOM!

WEEENDYYY...

YOU NEED TO CLE--

?!

MOMMY, I THINK SHE WON'T BE ABLE TO COME... SHE'S KISSIE-KISSING HER BOYFRIEND!

YOU SHOULD STOP WITH THE TOMATOES, Y'KNOW... YOU'RE STARTING TO LOOK LIKE THEM!

BWAH-HA

CAZENOVE & WILLIAM

CAZENOVE & WILLIAM

YOU'RE LUCKY YOU FOUND A BOYFRIEND...

...I'D REALLY LIKE TO HAVE ONE, TOO, Y'KNOW...

...BUT I THINK I'M TOO HARD TO PLEASE!

MY IDEAL BOYFRIEND SHOULD BE...

...EXTRA LOVING...

..AND CUDDLY AS ALL GET OUT... BUT REALLY FUNNY, TOO...

...AND HE SHOULD TELL ME HE LOVES ME EVERY DAY... AND NOT JUST ONCE...

LOL!

YEAH, WELL, I KNOW I'M ASKING FOR TOO MUCH...

OH, NO--NOT AT ALL!

I'LL LEND HIM TO YOU UNTIL YOU HAVE TIME TO GET YOURSELF ONE...THERE'RE TONS MORE IN THE TOY STORES!

GIVE ME A HUG!

I LOVE YOU!

HA HA

HA

56

CAZENOVE & WILLIAM

CAZENOVE & WILLIAM

CAZENOVE & WILLIAM

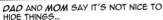
DAD AND MOM SAY IT'S NOT NICE TO HIDE THINGS...

THEY SAY THAT A FAULT CONFESSED IS HALF REDRESSED...

COME ON, MAUREEN-- GO FOR IT!

HEY, THERE... HEE-HEE...SAY, WENDY... UH, WEREN'T YOU LOOKING FOR ME?

NO, WHY?

WELL, 'CUZ I USED SCISSORS TO CUT UP YOUR FAVORITE PICTURE WITH MASON--EVEN THOUGH I DIDN'T DO IT ON-PURPOSE... WELL, NOT REALLY... WELL, MAYBE A LITTLE BIT.

ARE YOU MAD AT ME?

≑SIGH≑ I'M TOO OLD FOR THIS CHILDISHNESS, YOU KNOW...

...PLUS, I PICKED MY PRETTIEST TOP TO WEAR TO GO SHOPPING WITH AUDREY. SO DO YOU THINK I'M GOING TO SPOIL ALL THAT JUST TO JUMP ON YOU AND GIVE YOU A THRASHING?

THAT'S TRUE. YOU FORGIVE ME?

NO!

≑GASP!≑

IN YOUR DREAMS!

IN SHORT...DAD AND MOM JUST TALK NONSENSE!

CAZENOVE & WILLIAM

CAZENOVE & WILLIAM

THIS IS A SUPER POWERFUL TACTIC I SAW IN A MOVIE. IT WORKS EVERY TIME...

BABY BABY

LULU GETS **WENDY** TO BELIEVE I'M MEMORIZING HER PRIVATE DIARY...

THAT PEST!

≥GRRRR≤...

WENDY GOES UP TO HER ROOM AT FULL SPEED BUT IT'S **EMPTY**...

≥GRRRUMBLL≤...

WENDY CONFIRMS THAT HER BELOVED PRIVATE DIARY IS STILL IN ITS SUPER PRIVATE HIDING PLACE...

≥PHEW!≤

Diary

WENDY LEAVES, COMPLETELY REASSURED...

THEN I COME OUT FROM MY SUPER HIDEOUT UNDER THE BED, AND NOW I KNOW WHERE HER BELOVED DIARY IS!

NYUCK-NYUCK-NYUCK!

IT'S WORTH WATCHING TV SOMETIMES...

...TOO BAD I FORGOT I SAW THAT MOVIE WITH WENDY...

GOSSIP GIRL

Diary

61

CAZENOVE & WILLIAM

MAUREEN'S PICKED UP A NEW HABIT...

"CHUCKLING COW" OR "NULTELA" FOR MY SNACK.

EENIE, MEENIE, MINY, MOE...THUMP A TIGER ON THE TOE... WHEN HE THUMPS BACK DON'T BE SLOW.. EENIE, MEENIE, MINY, MOE!

CHOMP

IT'S THE SAME THING WHEN SHE'S CHOOSING A DVD.

EENIE, MEENIE, MINY, MOE...THUMP A TIGER ON THE TOE... IF HE THUMPS BACK...

...A COMICBOOK, TOO...

EENIE, MEENIE, MINY, MOE, THUMP A TIGER ON THE TOE, EENIE, MEENIE, MINY, MOE...

THRUM THRUM

HERE, MAUREEN, TRY IT WITH THIS.

WITH A QUARTER?

THERE'S NOTHING BETTER THAN HEADS OR TAILS FOR CHOOSING BETWEEN TWO OPTIONS, YOU KNOW.

OH, WELL. IT LANDED PERFECTLY. I WOULD'VE HAD TROUBLE CHOOSING BETWEEN LISTENING TO THIS CD BY KATY PUREE OR THIS OTHER ONE BY ISAYA.

SUPER COOL!

UH... ON THE OTHER HAND, SHOULD I LET IT ROLL OR TOSS IT INTO THE AIR?

HMM...

EENIE, MEENIE, MINY, MOE... THUMP A TIGER ON HIS TOE... EENIE, MEENIE, MINY MOE...

TROLLS

CAZENOVE & WILLIAM

WHAT'S THAT RACKET, *MAUREEN?*

DON'T KNOW, BUT IT'S A TOTAL *PAIN!*

NOOOO... A HERD OF *BOYS...*

...AND IN MY HOUSE, TOO!

WHY'S *WENDY* INVITING BOYS TO THE HOUSE? DOES SHE HAVE A SCREW LOOSE, OR WHAT?

PLUS BOYS AREN'T GOOD FOR ANYTHING...

...THEY'RE ALWAYS PLAYING FOOTBALL...

...OR NINTENDOX IN FRONT OF THE TV.

THEY DON'T SMELL GOOD...

...THEY'RE A BUNCH OF CROCKS LIKE SOCKS...

...THEY'RE NOISY...

...AND WORSE, THEY'RE *STRONGER* THAN GIRLS!

A-HA! THAT'S IT, *LULU!* WENDY'S GOING TO MOVE OUT AND SHE NEEDS LOTS OF GUYS TO HELP CARRY THE BOXES!

HEY, I'D REALLY LIKE TO HELP YOU WITH YOUR MOVE, BUT WHEN'RE YOUR FRIENDS GOING TO LEND *US* A HAND?

CAZENOVE & WILLIAM

SO, DO YOU KNOW IF *EMMA'S* COMING WITH US TO THE MOVIES?

NO, I NEED TO ASK HER.

I THOUGHT YOU'D SENT HER A TEXT.

NOT WORTH IT.

WHY? DOESN'T SHE HAVE HER CELL PHONE ANYMORE? DID HER PARENTS TAKE IT?

WHAT A TRAGEDY!

NO, IT'S NOT THAT.

IF NOT, WE COULD GO TO HER PLACE...

...SHE DOESN'T LIVE FAR FROM HERE.

DON'T WORRY ABOUT IT, *SAMMIE*. I'VE ACTUALLY GOT SOMETHING A LOT FASTER THAN THAT.

FASTER THAN AN SMS? WELL, LET'S SEE. YOU MUST THINK I'M AN *IDIOT*.

NO, OF COURSE NOT. IT'S CALLED AN "MSM"!

A WHAT?

≋PANT≋ ≋PANT≋ SO... ≋PHEW≋...I ALSO KNOW THAT WENDY AND SAMMIE WOULD LIKE TO KNOW IF YOU WANT TO GO...

...WITH THEM TO THE MOVIES... ≋PHEW≋...

AND SO ON AND SO FORTH...

AN "MSM": *MY SISTER MAUREEN!*

CAZENOVE & WILLIAM

≥PUFF≥...
ARE YOU SURE THEY PUT OUT LILIES OF THE VALLEY THIS YEAR?

LOL, SILLY! NO ONE PUTS THEM OUT...THEY GROW ON THEIR OWN!

WELL, OF COURSE THEY GROW. AND AROUND HERE, TOO.

THAT'S DUMB.

WE NEED TO SEARCH A LITTLE BETTER...

...THAT'S WHAT'S FUN ABOUT GATHERING LILIES OF THE VALLEY!

I'VE HAD ENOUGH FUN! I'M JUST GOING TO GATHER A BOUQUET OF GRASS FOR *MOM!*

THAT'LL BE JUST AS GOOD!

YOU'RE SO CRANKY, I SWEAR!

I TOLD YOU LILIES OF THE VALLEY ARE ALWAYS WELL-- HIDDEN...

...OTHERWISE IT'D BE TOO EASY...

...BUT WHAT--?

MAUREEEEN... HEY, COME BACK! I'LL HELP YOU...

FIVE MINUTES LATER...

NOW, LOOK HERE! WHAT'RE YOU DOING IN MY ROOM AGAIN, YOU SNOOP?!

EVERYTHING I REALLY WANT IS ALWAYS WELL-HIDDEN IN YOUR ROOM. SO THERE *MUST* BE SOME LILIES OF THE VALLEY HERE!

65

CAZENOVE & WILLIAM

CAZENOVE & WILLIAM

OOH, *RAPUNZEL*... YOUR HAIR'S AS BEAUTIFUL AS MY HORSE'S MANES.

TA-ĐAAAH, SUPER M...

YOU'RE SO SWEET, *FLYNN RIDER*...AND WHAT MUSCLES!

I'M SO IN LOVE WITH YOU.

KISS ME ON THE LIPS. YOU SMELL SO GOOD, ALMOST AS GOOD AS A JAR OF NULTELA.

UMM, YOU'RE DOING THE KISS WRONG, *LULU*.

FLYNN'S ARM SHOULDER HAS TO GO ONTO RAPUNZEL'S OTHER SHOULDER...

...THAT WAY SHE WON'T FALL BACKWARDS!

IT'S LIKE THIS ON TV, YOU SEE?!

WOOW!

IT DOESN'T WORK. LOOK, THEIR NOSES ARE TOUCHING!

WAIT...I'LL BE RIGHT BACK!

WENDY... WENDY...

WHEN YOU KISS *MASON* ON THE LIPS, WHERE DOES YOUR NOSE GO?

CAZENOVE & WILLIAM

I'M TELLING YOU IT'S NOT JUST A MIRROR. IT'S GOT TO BE A TV OR DVD PLAYER, TOO, I BET.

YEAH, WHICH EXPLAINS WHY MY SISTER SPENDS SO MANY HOURS IN FRONT OF IT!

CAZENOVE & WILLIAM

WHEN I CAME HOME FROM SCHOOL THIS AFTERNOON, I HAD A STRANGE SURPRISE...

HEYYY... HERE I AM...

I'M BACK FROM SCHOOL... I'M HUNGRY... I'M THIRSTY... OOOH, HEEEY...

NO ONE'S HERE TO WELCOME ME HOME? MY PARENTS DON'T HAVE SCHOOL!

UMM... MOM... WHY'RE YOU MEASURING MY BED? DID IT GROW, TOO?

WELL, YOU KNOW, SWEETHEART, IT'S BEEN A LONG TIME SINCE--

DON'T TELL ME YOU'RE GOING TO THROW IT OUT?!

MY BED HASN'T DONE ANYTHING TO YOU!

I'VE HAD IT SINCE I WAS LITTLE...

THE TWO OF US HAVE SO MANY MEMORIES TOGETHER!

OKAY, AS YOU WISH, MAUREEN.

WE WERE THINKING OF RE-DOING YOUR ROOM AND GETTING YOU A BIG BED. BUT IF YOU'D RATHER KEEP THIS ONE--

MAKE WAY... I'M BRINGING MY BOOKCASE AND MY DESK DOWN... COME ON, COME ON!

69

CAZENOVE & WILLIAM

MY NEW BED'S ANNOYING...

KREEE
CRAKK
EEEKRR

IT NEVER STOPS MAKING NOISE...

CREEE
EEECRAKK
CROOOAHK
EEEK

MOM SAYS IT'S THE WOOD WORKING ITSELF OUT...

CREEE
CREEESS
EEEEKKK

AS IF THIS WAS THE RIGHT TIME FOR WORKING OUT, HONESTLY...

GRUUL
CROOEEEK

WENDY, CAN I COME SLEEP WITH YOU? PRETTY PLEASE...?

MY BED WON'T STOP MAKING A BIG RACKET!

GNFR FRGNN GZZZ...

AT LEAST YOU DON'T HEAR WENDY'S BED...

SNORE ZZZ

BUT, I REALLY SHOULD THINK ABOUT EXCHANGING SISTERS!

SNOORE

SNOOOORE

CAZENOVE & WILLIAM

WHEN WE PLAY TENNIS, *MAUREEN'S* ALWAYS A SMART ALECK. THAT BUUUGS ME!

HEH-HEH. MY TURN TO *SERVE!*

LOOK! I'VE GOT MY *GAME FACE* ON!

15 *LOVE!*

DON'T YOU JUST TOTALLY *LOVE* THIS GAME?

LOVE LOVE LOVE LOVE LOVE

AND THERE YOU GO--I'M OVER THE NET!

HA HA HA

WATCH OUT, *WENDY!* NO MORE *SKIRTING* BY!

FINE, STOP BEING A *DIMWIT.*

CAN WE FINISH PLAYING ALREADY?!

FINE. ⸘PFFF⸘ YOU DON'T GET *ANY* OF MY *JOKES!*

POCK

BUT TENNIS IS REALLY *BORING!* LET'S SWITCH IT UP AND PLAY...

...*POOL!* YELLOW BALL IN THE SIDE POCKET!

CAZENOVE & WILLIAM

I LOOOVE MY NEW BEDDD!

ZBOING

IT'S SOOOO GREAT!

I LOVE LIFE!

IT'S SUPER-MEGA BIG...

YAHOO!

IT'S THE BESTEST BED IN THE WORLD!

WAIT, BUT MY BED'S BRAND NEW... I DON'T WANT TO WRECK IT BY JUMPING ON IT LIKE A MORON!

:RRRAAAH:.... WHAT'RE YOU DOING IN MY ROOM AGAIN?!

GET OUT... YOU'VE GOT 2 SECONDS TO CLEAR YOUR TOES OUT OF HERE!

YOU RODENT!

THE MARSUPA-MAUREEN IS GOING TO JUMP ON HER OWN BED LIKE A TRAMPOLINE!

CAZENOVE & WILLIAM

CAZENOVE & WILLIAM

CAZENOVE & WILLIAM

CAZENOVE & WILLIAM

I'M BORROWING A BUNCH OF YOUR STUFFED ANIMALS, WENDY!

THANKS!

OKAY, I GET IT...YOU'RE GETTING READY TO HAVE A GARAGE SALE, RIGHT?

NOT AT ALL! HANG ON, YOU CAN'T IMAGINE HOW MANY STUFFED ANIMALS IT TAKES TO COVER MY BIG NEW BED...

IT'S CRAZY!

CAZENOVE & WILLIAM

MAUREEN WAS A TOTAL PAIN AGAIN TODAY...

MOM, CAN I TAKE A BEGINNER'S HORSEBACK RIDING CLASS THIS AFTERNOON?

YES, OF COURSE, HONEY!

WOOW! THAT'S 'ZACTLY WHAT I WAS GOING TO ASK TO DO, TOO!

YAHOO!

I ADORE HORSE FACT FINDING... I WANT TO GO! I WANT TO GO! I WANT TO GO!

ANYWAY, SO I HAD TO DRAG MISS LEECH ALONG WITH ME TO THE PONY CLUB...

EQUESTRIAN CENTER

GALLOPING TRAIL

STABLES

DO YOU THINK THIS IS IT, WENDY?

OF COURSE, SHE HAD TO HAVE THE SAME EQUIPMENT AS ME...

NOW WE'RE REAL KNIGHTS!

THE SAME KIND OF HORSE...

IS THIS MY TWIN PONY? WHERE'D THE SECOND ONE GO?

AND THE SAME COURSE... LITTLE MISS POT O' GLUE ALL THE WAY THROUGH...

EVERYONE INTO THEIR SADDLES FOR A LITTLE WALK THROUGH THE WOODS.

AND RIGHT WHEN WE LEFT FOR THE WALK...

NO MORE MAUREEN...SHE DISAPPEARED...!

SHE MUST'VE SLIPPED AWAY!

77

CAZENOVE & WILLIAM

BABY BABY BABY OOH-HOO

HEY, *LAZY BONES*-- GET A MOVE ON, OKAY?!

≥ACK!≤ WAIT TWO MINUTES, PRETTY PLEASE...

...THERE'S SOME *THING-A-MA-JIGGY* IN THESE SKATES THAT'S BUGGING ME AND GIVING ME *HORROR-HIVES* TO ROLLERBLADE...

OKAY, OKAY, BUT STEP ON IT!

BUGS ME

BUUUUGGGGSSSS ME. ≥*AAARRRRGGGGH*≤...

I'M THE ONE YOU'RE BUGGING WITH ALL THIS WAITING! ARE YOU GOING TO BE DONE SOON?!

I'M A BIG GIRL NOW, I DON'T NEED TRAINING WHEELS ANY LONGER...

...THEY MADE ME FALL MORE THAN ANYTHING ELSE!

CLACK

CLACK

CAZENOVE & WILLIAM

CAZENOVE & WILLIAM

CAZENOVE & WILLIAM

HEY, *MAUREEN*, WHAT DO YOU THINK ABOUT US SPENDING THE DAY TOGETHER?

NOTHING BUT YOU AND ME.

REALLY? YOU AREN'T KIDDING?

WELL, NO! ARE WE SISTERS OR NOT?

IT'S SO STRANGE...EVER SINCE *WENDY'S* NO LONGER BEEN WITH *MASON*, SHE'S BEEN SUPER CLOSE TO ME...

DO YOU WANT MY POPCORN?

THIS FILM'S SO GOOD, DON'T YOU THINK?

SHHHH...

STRAWBERRY AND LEMON, MY FAVORITE FLAVORS.

MINE TOO. I LOVE THOSE THE BEST!

WE'VE TOLD EACH OTHER LOTS OF SECRETS AND ALL...

HA-HA-HA. YOU SHOULD'VE SEEN THE LOOK ON *AUDREY'S* FACE!

LOL!

BWAHAHA... TEE-HEE-HEE-HEE

KEEP FF THE RASS

...I ALMOST FELT AS IF I WAS PLAYING THE PART THAT MASON USED TO PLAY...

WHAT'LL WE DO NOW, WENDY?

LET'S GO SIT ON THE BENCH AGAIN.

MASON'S PART...

OKAY! BUT YOU'D BETTER NOT TRY TO GIVE ME AN *ICKY FRENCH KISS*, I'M WARNING YOU!

KEEP OFF THE GRASS

CAZENOVE & WILLIAM

CAZENOVE & WILLIAM

CAZENOVE & WILLIAM

LULU'S GOING TO HAVE A MEGA-BASH TONIGHT...

YAA-HOOOO!

I HAVE TO PRACTICE... I'VE PREPARED LOTS OF MEGA-TOP CDs!

MY GARBAGE BAG DANCE...

IT ROCKS!

STAIRWAY DANCE...

...SO AMAZING!

GARDEN HOSE DANCE...

DISHWASHING DANCE...

THAT EVENING...

SO, MAUREEN, YOU DON'T DANCE?

YES, BUT YOU WOULDN'T HAPPEN TO HAVE A GARBAGE CAN OR A STAIRWAY?

OR EVEN SOME DISHES TO WASH?

CAZENOVE & WILLIAM

YOU SHOULD BE SORRY, *MASON*...YOU STILL WENT OUT WITH MY BEST FRIEND...

UH-OH... SOMEONE'S IN *HOT WATER!*

BUT I CAN EXPLAIN, *WENDY.* ACTUALLY, I DIDN'T GO OUT WITH––

WELL, *YES,* BUT NO...

...SHE WAS ALREADY THERE AND... SINCE I WAS THERE, TOO...WELL, I, WE, US...

...I SWEAR I JUST WALKED HER HOME, SEE?!

YOU'RE THE ONE I LIKE, WENDY. I DON'T LIKE HER AT ALL, I SWEAR TO YOU...

WELL, OKAY, SHE'S NICE, TOO, BUT...NOT LIKE YOU ARE, Y'KNOW... I...

UM, DO YOU WANT SOMETHING TO DRINK, WENDY?

I...I'LL BE RIGHT BACK.

OOPS! HE'S HEADED THIS WAY!

WERE YOU LISTENING TO WHAT I WAS SAYING TO YOUR SISTER?!

HUH? WHAT SISTER?!

DO YOU WANT ME TO GIVE YOU A HAND WITH YOUR HOMEWORK?

NO, I'M FINE. BESIDES, YOU'RE WORTHLESS AT *EXPLANATIONING* ANYWAY!

CAZENOVE & WILLIAM

MAUREEN FINALLY DECIDED TO GO CLIMBING...

...AND CHOSE INDOOR BOULDERING...

SOMETHING FOR PROS, EH...

CLIPS

CLOPS

HEY! THAT'S MAUREEN OVER THERE!

YOO-HOO, MAAUREEENNN!

BEEP BEEP

WERE YOU IN THE FENCING CLASS? I DIDN'T SEE YOU

ROCK CLIMBING!

WOW! ROCK CLIMBING MUST BE GREAT!

‡PFFFF‡ I HATE IT.

BUT, WHY THE--

MAUREEEEEEN!

?

YOU BUSTED UP MY NINTENDOX AGAIN!

AH, OKAY... NOW I UNDERSTAND WHY YOU'RE ROCK CLIMBING...

YUP! IT'S A QUESTION OF SURVIVAL!

‡GRRRR‡...

‡af pizzas

ADAM

CAZENOVE & WILLIAM

STRANGE DAY TODAY...

FIRST, *MASON* CAME TO APOLOGIZE TO *WENDY* FOR GOING OUT WITH *SAMMIE*...

BOO-HOO-HOO-HOO-HOOO...

AFTER THAT, SAMMIE CAME TO ASK WENDY'S FORGIVENESS FOR STEALING HER BOYFRIEND...

SORRY-SORRY-SORRY...

SHE ALSO APOLOGIZED TO MASON...

YOU'RE SO GOOD TOGETHER...

AND AFTER THAT, WENDY ASKED SAMMIE AND MASON TO FORGIVE HER FOR SULKING...

I LOVE YOU BOTH!

⌇TSSSK⌇...YOU THREE REALLY ARE *IDIOTS*!

YOU'RE ALL *PATHETIC*.

WHY ON EARTH ARE YOU BEING SO MEAN, *MAUREEN*? WHY'D YOU SAY THAT?

JUST SO I COULD APOLOGIZE, TOO...

...I REALLY LOVE HUGS!

CAZENOVE & WILLIAM

MAUREEN'S TRIED EVERYTHING...

IF I WIN THE MATCH, YOU'LL GIVE ME MY BIRTHDAY PRESENT, OKAY?

NO WORRIES!

IF I GET THERE FIRST, CAN I HAVE IT?

DON'T WORRY...

WILL I GET MY PRESENT IF I GET A KING?

DON'T WORRY...

IF YOU MAKE FEWER BOUNCES THAN ME, I GET MY PRESENT!

THAT'S THREE ALREADY!

YES!

IF I BOUNCE HIGHER THAN YOU EVEN ONCE...

...I'LL GET MY PRESENT?!

- LOL!

...AND IT'S BEEN LIKE THAT EVERY DAY SINCE HER BIRTHDAY!

BUT THAT WAS THREE MONTHS AGO ALREADY?!

YOU'RE TAKING ADVANTAGE OF HER, WENDY!

SHE'S THE ONE WHO CARES ABOUT GETTING IT BY BEATING ME AT SOMETHING...

...BUT I THINK SHE'S GOING TO LET HERSELF GET IT NOW.

IF I'M SMALLER THAN YOU, I'LL GET MY PRESENT NOW?!

CAZENOVE & WILLIAM

CAZENOVE & WILLIAM

I LOVE GIVING *BIG HUGS*...

SURPRISE HUGS FOR *MOM* AND *DAD*, OF COURSE...

≷RAAAH≷ BUT-- ≷AARGH≷

...AND ALWAYS TO MY BEST BUDS...

UHM...THE TEACHER'S LOOKING AT US, *MAUREEN*...

...TO MY BUDS' BOYFRIEND...

I SWEAR I'VE GOT NOTHING TO DO WITH IT. SHE'S THE ONE WHO--

...TO MY SISTER'S BUDS...

WHOA, THERE! THIS IS GETTING *STRANGE*...

WITH *WENDY*, I HAVE TO BE CUNNING. SHE ISN'T ALSWAY OKAY WITH BIG HUGS...

THE MAIL'S HERE...

OOOH... A TEEN MAG...

AND SINCE SHE CAN'T STAND FOR ME TO READ IT FIRST...

DON'T TOUCH MY MAGAZINE!

AND THERE IT IS--A BIG HUG ANYWAY!

CAZENOVE & WILLIAM

SPECIALTY OF *CHEF MAUREEN:* "SUPER DELICIOUS COOKIES!"

THEY'LL MAKE YOU FORGET *MASON*, YOU'LL SEE....

MMM, THANKS.

THERE'S LOTS OF THINGS IN 'EM. YOU'RE *SOOO* GOING TO LOVE 'EM.

OH, GEEZ. IT TASTES LIKE FEET.

YUCK!

THEY'VE GOT CHOCOLATE, BRIE, AND LETTUCE FOR COLOR...

I'LL BRING OUT THE NEXT ONE.

TA-DAAAH!

TOMATO CAKES. I KNOW YOU LOVE THEM BUT I DIDN'T BAKE IT 'CUZ I PREFER RAW DOUGH...

HOW ABOUT A *HOUSE COCKTAIL* TO HELP EVERYTHING GO DOWN...

I PUT IN EVERYTHING I FOUND IN THE FRIDGE-- APPLES, ZUCCHINI, CAULIFLOWER...

TOMORROW, I'LL MAKE YOU A *FLOWER PIE...*

...I FOUND THE RECIPE IN A COMIC- BOOK.

UGH!

REALLY, *WENDY?* YOU'D LIKE TO GO OUT WITH ME AGAIN, TOMORROW?

WELL, YES, I'D LIKE TO VERY MUCH...

...MY STOMACH'S COUNTING ON IT!

CAZENOVE & WILLIAM

HEY, *WENDY*, DO YOU REMEMBER HOW I STUCK TO YOU WHEN WE WERE LITTLE...

...WORSE THAN A PIECE OF CHEWING GUM ON THE BOTTOM OF A SNEAKER?

I'D SAY A *LEECH*, INSTEAD.

REMEMBER WHEN I USED TO HIDE MYSELF BEHIND A BUSH TO WATCH YOU FLIRT?

AND YOU THOUGHT WE DIDN'T SEE YOU, ⸯTSSSK⸰...

SLICE SLICE

BANG

AND WHEN I USED TO WORM MY WAY BETWEEN THE TWO OF YOU AT THE MOVIES...

LOL, YOU'D MAKE ONE OF THOSE FACES EVERY TIME!

AND YOU WOULD SAY IT WAS JUST TO KEEP FROM GETTING COLD.

ONE TIME I EVEN I HID A WALKIE-TALKIE UNDER YOUR PILLOW...

...SO I COULD HEAR EVERYTHING YOU BABBLED TO YOUR BOYFRIEND ON THE PHONE.

HA! YOUR WALKIE-TALKIE WOUND UP IN THE GARBAGE CAN!

HEE-HEE... WHEN I THINK ABOUT IT, I WAS PRETTY CLOSE TO BEING A *PEST*, A *LEECH*, A *SNOOP*, A *GATECRASHER*...

ANYWAY, ARE YOU HAVING SOMETHING GOOD TO EAT WITH *MASON*? I'M ABSOLUTELY STARVING!

ⸯMMPH⸰...

IT'S A CURSE. WE'LL *NEVER, EVER* BE ALONE--JUST THE TWO OF US!

92

CAZENOVE & WILLIAM

WATCH OUT FOR PAPERCUTᴢ™

Welcome to the thrilling third THE SISTERS graphic novel, featuring those testy tween(ish) terrors, Wendy and Maureen, by Christophe Cazenove and William Maury, from Papercutz—that pseudo dysfunctional faux-family dedicated to publishing great graphic novels for all ages. I'm Jim Salicrup, the Editor-in-Chief and Honorary Third Sister, and I'm here to take you behind-the-scenes at Papercutz and tell you about our most exciting new project...

Papercutz is launching not just one all-new graphic novel series, not just two all-new graphic novel series, but an entire new <u>line</u> of graphic novels created just for you! That is if you're interested in graphic novels featuring great characters, in amazing situations, having awesome adventures, with a touch of romance. If so, Charmz is just what you've been looking for! Charmz, the all-new imprint from Papercutz. And here's a list of the first few Charmz graphic novels...

CHED Copyright © 2017 Mariah
Court and Aaron Alexovich.

First up is STITCHED, by Mariah McCourt, writer (and Charmz Editor), and Aaron Alexovich, artist. STITCHED is a supernatural tale about Crimson Volania Mulch, a rag-doll girl who wakes up in a cemetery, but doesn't know anything except her name. Her first few nights "alive" are a spooky whirlwind of ghosts, werewolves, witches, and weirdly-beautiful boys. Will she find out where she comes from? Do two-headed badger/hedgehogs eat cupcakes? Does Crimson even have time for romance when she doesn't even know who she is? Or does she have to fall apart before she can be whole again?

Next there's SWEETIES, based on Cathy Cassidy's novel *The Chocolate Box Girls*, adapted by Véronique Grisseaux, writer, and Anna Merli, artist. SWEETIES is about blending two families into one. Cherry acquires four half-sisters, Honey, Skye, Summer, and Coco, when her candy-making father Paddy marries their mother, Charlotte. Things get complicated when Cherry falls for Honey's boyfriend and Skye falls in love with the man of her dreams – literally!

Filles au Chocolat [SWEETIES] Copyright
014, 2015, 2017 Jungle! The Chocolate Box
s © 2010, 2011, 2017 by Cathy Cassidy.

Finally (for now) there's CHLOE, by Greg Tessier, writer, and Amandine, co-writer and artist. Chloe Blin is determined to be popular, confident, and in love! Unfortunately she has to deal with mean girl cliques, fashion faux pas, and trying to impress the cutest boy in school with her sweet moves... only to fall completely flat. Whether it's rocking a party that goes sideways or making the best of a less than ideal vacation, Chloe may not always get it right at first, but she doesn't give up!

Charmz editor Mariah McCourt wants these graphic novels to be "the book equivalent of a hot chocolate; sweet, maybe a little dark sometimes, comforting, and made just for you. You can curl up with our tales, settle in, and enjoy falling in love with our characters just like they fall in love with each other."

To get a better idea what these graphic novels are like, check out the special preview pages of STITCHED, SWEETIES, and CHLOE on the following pages. The graphic novels are available now at booksellers and libraries everywhere.

For more information, and more sneak previews of Charmz titles, and all the latest Papercutz news, be sure to visit us at papercutz.com. And don't forget to contact us an let us know what you think of everything we're up to! We also suspect you won't want to miss THE SISTERS #4 "Selfie-Awareness," coming soon to those very same wonderful booksellers and libraries!

Thanks,

Jim

STAY IN TOUCH!

EMAIL: salicrup@papercutz.com
WEB: www.papercutz.com
TWITTER: @papercutzgn
INSTAGRAM: @papercutzgn
FACEBOOK: PAPERCUTZGRAPHICNOVELS
REGULAR MAIL: Papercutz, 160 Broadway, Suite 700, East Wing, New York, NY 10038

stinguette [CHLOE] Copyright © 2011, 2012, 2017 Jungle!

GLASGOW, SCOTLAND. CLYDE ACADEMY.

CAN'T LIE.

THERE ARE SOME THINGS I'LL MISS ABOUT CLYDE ACADEMY.

LIKE THIS *DELIGHTFUL* LUNCH FOOD.

OR STARING AT THE BACK OF RYAN CLEGG'S... NECK.

THERE ARE ALSO THINGS I WILL *NOT* MISS:

LIKE MATH TESTS AND--

KIRSTY McRAE!

SHE AND HER FRIENDS DRIVE ME CRAZY!

EXCUSE ME, CHERRY COSTELLO!

WE NEED SOME MORE ROOM.

WAP

HEY, GIRLS!

DID YOU KNOW, CHERRY'S MUM THOUGHT SHE WAS SUCH A *LOSER* THAT SHE DITCHED HER AND RAN OFF TO LIVE ON THE OTHER SIDE OF THE WORLD?

YOU DON'T KNOW ANYTHING ABOUT MY MUM!

An evening before school starts up, in an ordinary, small town.

IT'S HARD TO BE THE NEW GIRL.

I HOPE I CAN MAKE MYSELF SOME NEW, COOL, FRIENDS. RIGHT, CARTOON?

IT'S TIME TO GO TO BED!

QUIET DOWN, I KNOW WHAT TIME IT IS! DON'T COME IN MY ROOM!

I WILL IF I WANNA!

IF I WANNA!

IF I WANNA!

STOP!

CALM DOWN IN HERE! ARTHUR, LEAVE YOUR SISTER CHLOE ALONE. SHE'S GOT ENOUGH STRESS WITHOUT YOU ADDING TO IT!

COME ON OUT AND NO ARGUING!

SWEET DREAMS, LITTLE MISTY!

GOOD-NIGHT, MOM.